# The
# Princess
# Knight

First published in Germany by Fischer Taschenbuch Verlag GmbH © 2001

Published in the United Kingdom in 2003 by The Chicken House, 2 Palmer Street, Frome, Somerset, BA 11 1DS.
Email: *chickenhouse@doublecluck.com*

Library of Congress Cataloging-in-Publication data available
Reinforced Binding for Library Use

ISBN 0-439-53630-8

10 9 8 7 6 5 4 3 2 1                                                          04 05 06 07 08
Printed in Mexico      49
First American edition, March 2004

# The Princess Knight

By
Cornelia Funke

*Illustrations by*
Kerstin Meyer

*Translated by* Anthea Bell

The Chicken House
SCHOLASTIC INC.
New York

King Wilfred the Worthy had three sons.
He brought them up just as his father had brought *him* up,
and they were taught all the things *he* had been taught.
He wanted them to be better than his best knights.

They learned riding and jousting, fighting with swords, and good table manners, too.

They learned how to stride around proudly and how to shout *very* loudly.

And (perhaps most important for princes) they learned how to give orders — to their nursemaids, their servants, their dogs, and their horses.

Then Queen Violetta had a
daughter. But the queen died when the
baby was born. So, the little girl was
called Violetta.

No one would dare tell the king *how* to do anything —
especially how to raise his little girl. So he decided to teach
her the same lessons that he had taught his sons . . .

even though she was so small
she could hardly lift a sword at all!

Her brothers teased her and called her names.
"Itsy-Bitsy Little Vi — little girl can't hurt a fly!"

And they would boast that
they were so strong, even
the most spirited horse
would obey them.

Then they'd strike the heads off practice dummies
so hard that the heads would fly right over the
castle walls!

And they would laugh and laugh at their little sister
as she struggled to mount a horse in her heavy armor,
as if it were the funniest thing they'd ever seen.

"Oh, Emma," said Violetta to her nursemaid one evening, while Emma soothed the little girl's bruises. "I'll never be as strong as my brothers."

"Not as strong, maybe, but you are three times as clever," said Emma sensibly. "Why not ask your father to stop teaching you all this silly fighting and to let you learn something else instead? Embroidery perhaps. Or weaving. Or playing the flute. Something *useful?*"

But Violetta shook her head.

"No, no, no," she said. "That would only make my brothers laugh louder."

So Emma said no more. For she knew the princess was more determined than all the three princes put together.

From that night on, Violetta slipped out of the castle in secret, while the rose gardener's son kept watch for her.

She started to practice all the things her brothers could already do so much better.

Violetta practiced in her own way, without shouting and without using her spurs.

Indeed, she was very quiet about it — as quiet as the night itself.

So, while her brothers grew as tall and strong as
King Wilfred's knights, Violetta, who stayed quite small,
got better at fighting and riding every day. And her father's
horses loved to carry her on their backs.

Violetta became so nimble and quick that when her three
brothers practiced jousting with her, their spears and swords
just hit the empty air. And the princes soon stopped
laughing at her. And they stopped calling her
"Itsy-Bitsy Little Vi!"

Then came the day before Violetta's sixteenth birthday, and the king asked to see her.

"Violetta," said King Wilfred, "I'm going to hold a jousting tournament in honor of your birthday. The victory prize will bring the bravest knights in the land flocking to the castle."

"What will that prize be, Father?" asked Violetta, wondering which horse she would ride, which of her suits of armor would be lightest, and which plume she would wear in her helmet.

"The prize," said King Wilfred, "will be your hand
in marriage. So put on your finest gown
and practice your prettiest smile."

Violetta turned as red as the roses beside the castle moat. "What!" she cried. "You want *me* to marry some dimwit in a tin suit? Just look at your own knights! They whip their horses and they can't even write their own names!"

Her father was so angry that he locked Violetta up in the castle tower all by herself. Not until the moon was shining high in the sky did the King tell Violetta's youngest brother to let her out.

"Stop crying, little sister!" said Violetta's brother. "I'll make sure to win the tournament myself. You certainly can't marry *me!*"

But Violetta shook her head and wiped her eyes on the hem of her dress.

"Thank you," she said, "but I think I'd better just see to it myself."

The next day the field behind the castle was crowded
with knights who had come to fight in the tournament.
King Wilfred sat down to watch. Little did he know that
it wasn't Violetta who sat beside him. It was her nursemaid,
Emma. She wore Violetta's best dress and a veil over her face.

The real Violetta had put on her blackest armor and saddled her favorite horse. She rode into the arena with the other knights and gave her title as Sir No-Name.

Trumpets sounded and the tournament to win the princess's hand began. Knight after knight rode into the arena — Sigurd the Strong, Harold the Hardy, Percy the Pitiless — but Sir No-Name defeated them all. He even knocked the king's sons off their horses and into the dust.

By the end there was no one left who was willing to fight.
And Sir No-Name rode over to the king to receive
the victory prize.

"Where do you come from, Sir No-Name?" asked the king. "You have brought honor to your family, and my daughter should think herself lucky to take your hand in marriage."

"Oh, I don't think so!" Sir No-Name replied, raising his helmet . . .

"Hello, Father," said Violetta. "What's the prize for a *Princess* Knight?"

And for the first time in his life, her father, the king, was speechless.

Violetta turned to the defeated knights, sitting battered
and bruised on their horses.

"Very well," she said. "I shall choose my own prize."

"I hereby proclaim that no one will ever win Princess Violetta's hand in marriage without first defeating Sir No-Name."

Then she turned on her horse and rode away — far, far away. And she didn't return for a year and a day.

And when she did? Why, her father, King Wilfred the Worthy, gave her a horse as black as her armor. And nobody, not even her brothers, challenged the princess ever again.

And who *did* she marry? Well, if you must know, many years later, she married the rose gardener's son and lived happily ever after.